NOTE: It seems not only does Alexandra ramble on, so does the publisher (**ahem**!) Hmm.

ALEXANDRA! Rambles On!

ONE PUPPY, THREE TALES

by Karen Salmansohn

SCHOLASTIC INC.

New York   Toronto   London   Auckland   Sydney
Mexico City   New Delhi   Hong Kong   Buenos Aires

There are **many things** I'm still waiting for **my dad** to tell me.

For example:

Why can **dogs** understand our language, but we can't understand theirs?

Does a **parrot** really know what it is saying when it talks? And does **my brother, Howie,** really know what he is saying when he talks? And if so, why does he say so many stupid things?

My mom loves it when I ask her questions like these. She answers me

BOW WOW.

TRANSLATION: Is the speed of the ball affected more by its weight or size?

Polly wants a cracker.

TRANSLATION: Polly REALLY wants a pizza, but will settle for a stale cracker.

in a **MOM-o-Logue**. But every time I ask my dad a question, he gives me the **same answer**: "I'm very busy right now, Alexandra, I'll talk to you later."

Which brings me to some **NEW** questions.

Some NEW Questions:

. When is **later** anyway?

. Is it sooner than a **fortnight**?

. Less than a **fortmorning**?

. And what are those, anyway?

. Will later ever come?

. Will it come by the time I reach **age 13** ...or **page 49**?

• Why is dad spelled backward still dad— and mom still mom—but brother is **rehtorb**?

TALE #1

What is weird? Weird is what?

It is now **7:03** P.M. Do you know where your mother is? • I don't. • My mom was supposed to be home at 6 P.M. — one hour ago — or four bracelets in "bracelet-making time." (Note: That's how many bracelets I've beaded since waiting for her.) • Right now I am in my room, putting the last little pink bead on this fourth bracelet (an orange and pink one) and wondering where my mom could be. She promised me she'd be home from rehearsal early tonight — with my Halloween costume — because I have this cool Halloween party that I am **SUPPOSED TO BE AT — IN UNDER**

CHOCOLATE

achem!

LATE as in what my mom is!

HAPPY PUMP-KIN!

BLUE PUMP-KIN?

Grrr rrrr rrrr rrrr rrrr rr

MOM ← hopefully heading this way →

HOME

ONE HOUR! • Yikes! • **Where** is my mom with my costume already?! • Okay. I am giving my mom two more bracelets to get here before I get really mad — like Grrrrr mad. I decide to make this next bracelet orange and black in honor of Halloween. I love Halloween — and not just for the **FREE CHOCOLATE** (yum!). But also the way I see it, any day where I get to be someone **other than myself** is fine by me. • This year I found my favorite Halloween costume ever: **a glamourous movie star costume!**

PARTY

1

hour

another?

ME → WITHOUT costume

pink bead

Bracelet

And my favorite part of getting to be a movie star is (no, not the rhine-stone studded sunglasses!) – the **HAIR!** I am going to get to wear this cool wig of **long straight blond hair.** Real movie star hair. • My real hair is more of the peasant sort: dark, curly, and very moody. • Every morning when I wake up, I look in the mirror nervously, scared of what personality my hair will take on for that day. If my hair has decided to be super curly (meaning super weirdo) I find myself totally dreading school. • My mother's hair is like mine. She tells me, "You know, there are people out there who pay lots of money to have hair like ours. Some day — just like me — you'll be glad to have curly hair." • **Puh-lease.** • Vicki Stone, the girl who invited me to tonight's cool Halloween party, has the hair I dream of having — blond, straight hair so **SHINY** you'd think you could see yourself in it, if you stood in front of it and stared really hard. Vicki, in my opinion, is the coolest girl in school. She looks **like an ad for Perfect Girl Shampoo.**

• And not only is Vicki really cool, so is Vicki's mom. • I met Vicki's mom at this year's school fund-raiser. She—like Vicki—has that beautiful hair. Plus she dressed very classy, in this pretty navy suit, and she baked theee best **Lemon Meltaways** ever—perfect amounts of lemoniness and meltability. EVERYTHING about Vicki's mom is as perfect as her meltaways—and as opposite from MY mom as you can get.

• My mom showed up that day ... and looking so..., so... so... NON-mom-ish. • First of all, there's her totally NON-mom hair. • Next of all, she wore this ver NON-mom outfit — a black leotard top and this weird **zebra print** skirt. I ask you: What kind of mom wears **zebra?**

LATE as usua

And OF COURSE mom did not bake anything for the fundraiser. Instead, she set up a table where she offered to teach people...

... YOGA! My mom (GET THIS...) then took off her **zebra** skirt and stood there wearing only a black leotard yoga outfit. (How embarassing, right?) Then she twisted herself into...

... weird yoga positions and tried to get people to sign up with her so she could show **them** how to twist into weird positions, too. • She kept shouting things like, "Okay, bring on the next victim!" really, really **LOUDLY.** It was soooo embarrassing! I swear, I turned the color of these beads right here! (uh-oh! I'm now starting bracelet #2! **WHERE IS SHE?)**

Mom's big problem: She does not know how to ac
her age.

"I still feel like a teenager," my mom insists.
"I don't feel like a mom."

My mom has even told me she doesn't want me
to think of her as "**my mom**" but as "**my friend**."
But I don't want a mom who is my friend. A
mom is supposed to be **A MOM**. It's sort of
like how you would not want to use a lamp
as a **chair** or a **pencil** as an **umbrella**. My
mom insists she cannot stop herself from
acting non-mom-ish — all **loud** and **goofy** and
embarrassing.

"I'm a **cabaret lounge singer**," she explains

Huh? As if **that's** an explanation!

Note: What that means is that my mom sings songs, not while standing, like a **normal person**, but while **sitting on top of a piano.** She calls herself a "**CROONER**" which I guess means "a person who sings songs while sitting on top of a piano."

"The breeze is chasing the zephyr," mom croons. "The moon is chasing the sea, the bull is chasing the heifer, but nobody's chasing me."

Note to mom: Maybe nobody's chasing you because you're wearing a **dorky zebra print outfit.**

I don't mean to be mean. But I'm mad at my mom for being **sooo late** with my costume—and for being **so embarrassing!** I hate having **Zebra MoM** come to meet me at school.

zebra
from
ze front

I've read a lot about zebras, and let me tell you: **zebras are very weird animals**. Not only do no two zebras look alike, no two act alike.

Some people think zebras are just like horses with stripes. But they are **very different**. Zebras are more wild and less open to suggestion from others. A zebra will only do what the zebra itself wants to do. That's why a horse can be trained, but a zebra cannot. And that's why you hear about **Horse Whisperers** but not Zebra Whisperers.

(**Question**: If a Horse Whisperer is a person who speaks with horses, would a **Horse Crooner** be a person who speaks to horses while sitting on a piano?)

Anyway, I often wish I had **a normal Horse Mom** - like Vicki's mom - a mom who is sleek and graceful and gets along well with others. Instead I got stuck with **Zebra Mom**, who bugs me and embarrasses me.

Zebra from ze rear

SOME STUFF THAT BUGS ME AND EMBARRASSES ME ABOUT MY MOM:

① (Or rather, make that number ⑥, because I think I already listed about 5 things, so it's...)

⑥ my mom is always doing spacey stuff, like slipping up and calling me "Howie." (**Note:** I get back at her by calling her "Dad.")

⑦ My mom is always confusing me with her. she hates tomatoes, so I must hate tomatoes. She loves zebra print, so I must love zebra print. Once she even got me weird zebra print shoes, then expected me to wear them!

"mom, puh-lease," I told her. "They are like so weird."
• "I know," said my mom, "Aren't they just great?" Basically, my mom just does not get it.

WEIRD DOES NOT = GREAT. Weird = being not normal. And what I want = being normal. What I want = a mom who = **a mom!**

my best friend, Liz, tells me I should appreciate my mom just as she is. Liz thinks my mom is VERY cool. But I think that's because:

① my mom once told Liz she looks like Winona Ryder– and **Liz loves Winona.** Liz even named her cat Winona.

② Liz doesn't have a mom at all. Liz's mom passed away when she was seven. So my mom has sort of become Liz's replacement mom.

• Liz is my **VBF** - my **Very Best Friend**. And Liz is not only close to me, she's also **CLOSE TO ME**. She lives right next door. I love that I have Liz so close by to talk to - and that I can talk to Liz about **ANYTHING** and not feel like she is looking at me like I have smudged ink all over my face. • Liz and I talk about **EVERYTHING**. stuff like:

① Liz's **crush** on this boy, **Karl**.
② my **crush** on this boy, **max**.
③ who we think is **cool** and **pretty** and **why**.

• I think Vicki is the prettiest and coolest girl in our school - and her mom is the most coolest mom ever. • "you and your mom are wa-aay cooler," Liz has told me. "I think Vicki and her mom are BOTH totally **BORING!**". • But I think Liz just told me that because:

① mom said that Winona Ryder look-a-like thing.
② Vicki **did not invite** Liz to her Halloween party.

• Liz claims she did not want to go to Vicki's "**STUPID**" (Note: That's **Liz's word**) party. • "It's probably going to be very boring," Liz has said, "just like Vicki and her boring mom.". • But I don't know... I **doubt** Liz thinks that **FOR REAL**.

I just think Liz is **jealous** that I am going to Vicki's party - that is if I am **ever** going. I'm almost done with this second bracelet, and my mom—what that? Could it be? • Yes! **FINALLY**, mom is coming through the front door. It took 5 ½ bracelets, but **FINALLY**, she's home. • "Who wants ice cream?" my mom yells. • "Yeah!" my dad and Howie both yell back from the living room where they are watching a basketball game. • We all run into the kitchen to greet

MY NEW COSTUME

NOTHING

my mom, who is standing there **WITH** ice cream but **WITHOUT** costume! • "Where is my costume?" • "What?" says my mom. "I'm so sorry, honey. Rehearsal ran late, then I totally forgot. • What I am thinking is: Grrrrrr. • What comes out of my mouth is: "mom! How could you? Now the store is closed and I have

NOTHING to wear to Vicki's party. Now I can't go!!". "I'm so sorry, honey," says my mom. "you want to go see a movie instead?". "I do," says my brother. • "That's a great idea," says my dad. • What I am now thinking is: Grrrr r r r r r r r r r r r r r r r r - r r r r r r r r r r r r r r r r r r r r - r r r r r - r r r r r!•"

MY NEW MOOD
DARK

I don't want to SEE movie stars, I want to dress up like one!" I say, then run to my room and slam the door really, really loudly. I am so angry! Should I go to Vicki's party without a costume or should I not go to Vicki's party at all? I think about calling Liz. But I know what she'll say: "Why would you even want to go to Vicki's **stupid** party anyway?" But I **DO** want to go. I **REALLY** want to go. And so I'm **REALLY** angry at mom.• I hear a **KNOCK**.

"Honey," says my mom. • "Don't come in," I say. • The door opens ANYWAY. • Grrrrr. "Look what I found," says my mom, sticking her **brightly colored Japanese bathrobe** in my face. • "Why are you showing me your robe?" I ask. • "It's your new **geisha girl costume**," says my mom. "For Vicki's party. And we could **paint your face white, and stick chopsticks in your hair**". "I...er...". • "Try it on," says my mom. • I take off my sweats...and slip on her Japanese robe. Before I can say anything, my mom starts powdering my face with lots of makeup. I stare at myself in the mirror. In the end I think I look **kind of sort of kind of maybe** pretty cool. • "So?" says mom, smiling this big goofy smile—the kind of smile you get when you stick a quarter of an orange in your mouth. • "So, what do you think?" she asks. • "I think maybe I'll go to Vicki's party after all." • My mom tries to put her arms around me, but I push her off. • "However," I say, "I ALSO think that I am STILL mad at you—and will be—for at least **six more bracelets**." • "What?" says my mom. • "Never mind," I say. "Let's go." • " My mom and I head to the car, where my brother and dad are already waiting. They drop me off at Vicki's house on their way to the movies. • "see you afterwards,

darling!" my mom yells and waves as they drive off.
• Vicki has a pretty house (duh! of course!) with lots
of white, and a pretty powder blue door. I ring Vicki's
doorbell. (It even makes a pretty ding dong sound.) •
Vicki's mom answers. • "Yes, can I help you?" she asks.
• "I'm here for the Halloween party," I explain. • "The
Halloween party?" • "Am I early?" • "Late, dear. I'm
afraid the party was yesterday." • "Yesterday?," I
repeat. • **How did this happen?** Did my mom write the
party down on the calendar in the **WRONG SPACE?** Did
I space and tell my mom the **WRONG** date? Am I
becoming as ditzy as my mom? **WHO** should I be mad
at? Me? Or my mom? • I decide either way I should
be mad at my mom, because my mom is slowly and
sneakily turning me into her. Yes, I am becoming my
mom. Yes, THIS, it seems is now my new Halloween costume.
• "Oh, well," I say and try to smile. • My **NEW** goal for
the moment: look cool, calm, and collected. My **NEW**
goal for life: I will not turn into my spacey, weird
mom. **I will not turn into my spacey weird mom.**
• Though it's hard to look cool, calm, and collected
(or nonspacey and nonweird) while one is dressed like a
geisha girl on someone's doorstep. • (Somebody kill
me now, please!) • "Well, sweetie," Vicki's mom
says, "Vicki is out with her dad. Why don't you
call your mom and have her pick you up?" • "my
mom's not home," I say. "Nobody is. They all
went to a movie. They won't be home for, like,

two hours." • "Oh, too bad Vicki isn't here. Bu
come in." • I look at Vicki's mom's sweet
face and think how much I wish Vicki's
normal mom were **MY** mom. I wish I had a
NORMAL mom **FOREVER**. • She brings me into the
kitchen where there are two other women —
two other normal mom types - seated at a
big round table. I have hit the **normal mom**
jackpot! Both   these new
normal moms   are wearing
pretty blue   **NORMAL**
dresses —   like real mom:
— with not a   zebra stripe
in sight. • "Her   mother con-
fused the day   of the party,
Vicki's mom   explains. • "Oh
dear," says one of   the normal moms.
• I happily take a seat next to Vicki's mom.
On the table is a plate of her **lemon melt-**
aways. Together all four of us sit, eat
meltaways, watch TV, and talk recipes. Or
at least three out of four of us talk recipes,
while one of us (me!) just listens to: oven
preheating recommendations, favorite
ingredients, and the difference between
Pyrex and Stonewall baking dishes. **That's**
when I discover what normal moms really

A MOUTH EATING A LEMON MELTAWAY

think/say. And what I discover is: Normal moms are **really boring.** • "I always add a teaspoon of baking soda to my cornbread," says one normal mom. • "Really!" the others gasp. • "I like to mix in brown sugar with white sugar in my sugar cookies," says another normal

mom. • "My, how clever!" one says. • "What a great idea!" says another. • **As if!** • I look at the clock, and suddenly I cannot **wait** for my two hours to pass. These two hours now seem like a life- time. That's when I wonder:

What would a lifetime with a normal mom feel like? Just the thought of this makes me thirsty. • "Excuse me, Mrs. Stone," I say to Vicki's mom. "Can I please have some more juice?" • "I'm Mrs. White," the woman answers. "That's Mrs. Stone, over there." • I look at them both, then at the

...third woman, and I can't tell any of the three normal moms apart. They all look so much alike. Like

b. one big blue blur.

I watch them, watch me, and as they now I see how they all even raise their drinking glasses at the same time! • Suddenly, instead of seeing these women as Horse Moms - acting like a sleek pack of horses - I see them all as ants - like ants on a hillside, ants that all look the same, and all do the same ant things, all together.

I've read a lot about
ant behavior.
It is called
"Alleo Mimetic Behavior" and it means:

"When animals in a group
all start to think and
behave in the same way."

Alleomimetic Behavior
means: There are no
unique thinkers or
doers in the
group.

No one ant
is capable of thinking
or doing something unique
that it likes,
like yoga or sitting on top
of pianos crooning.

An ant
just does what everybody else
is doing just because
everybody else is
doing it.

How boring
is that?

Then I think:
          MAYBE Liz is right.
MAYBE
     I should **be glad to have**
     a Zebra Mom...

and not some...

          ...Alleomimetic Ant Mom.

when those two hours finally pass
          and my mom actually shows up, I
am actually glad to see her
          FOR A CHANGE.

               ...I am
          EVEN actually
               sort of maybe
          even kinda glad to see
               her **zebra**
                    coat.

          Later that
               night
          when
               I get home,
     I pull out all the
black and white   and I make
beads I have,   my mom the
                                   prettiest,
                         coolest, niftiest
     black and white bracelet EVER.

MICRO COSMIC CHAPTER

Another Question:

Why were big, huge **DINOSAURS** not able to survive the test of time, but teeny, tiny termites were? Yes, **termites** have been around since the time of dinosaurs. meaning? A termite is harder to kill than a dinosaur. It seems a teeny termite is **very strong!** It can chew through houses and trees— and maybe even dinosaurs! And if you try to poison a termite, it has this **super strong tummy** that can resist most poisons! **(QUESTION:** Shouldn't termite be spelled **"TERMIGHT"**?) Probably if you tried to poison a huge dinosaur, it would fall over and **become history** which I guess explains why dinosaurs **are** history, and termites are **not**. But there is one way for sure to kill a termite. Here it is. **HOW TO KILL A TERMITE:** Take the termite away from its other termite friends. Then the termite will die. **IT'S LIKE THIS:** A termite gets a lot of its strength and energy from being around other termites. It needs to be around **its friends** or else it won't have the energy to flutter its wings. It will just sit there until it **dies.** Even just having **one friend** next to it gives it some strength to **fly!** I relate. That's the way I feel about Liz. Whenever Liz is around, I always feel **more fluttery.** Once when I was home sick, Liz came by to visit, and because she was sitting next to me on the bed, I suddenly felt a lot more energetic, which is something that would happen to a sick termite if a termite came near it. Sometimes, all I have to do is see Liz and I feel all fluttery.

Note #1: These dots are termites eating a yummy dino-snack.

Note #2: No dinosaurs were hurt or killed in the making of this drawing!

TALE #2

FREE TO BE ME
...or does being me have a price?
and if so, how much should I charge?

Note: see the happy face? I drew Liz upside down so she would look like she's smiling even though she's unhappy.

Liz and I have now started our own jewelry business. • Liz and I love making **beaded bracelets, necklaces, earrings, and rings**, which everyone is always complimenting us on sooo much— and asking us if they can buy them from us— well, Liz and I decided we should sell OUR jewelry during lunchtime. • So we are. • And... we've already sold **19 pieces!** OUR **BIG PLAN**: Make enough money to buy ourselves computers! • **OUR BIGGER PLAN**: Set up a web site and sell our jewelry on the **Internet**! • How amazing would that be? huh? • And just last week Vicki told me how much she loved my bracelets—

and how much she wanted one - a pink and orange one, like the one I was wearing. She tried it on and it fit her perfectly so I told her she could have it. She asked if she could have it for **free** since it was kinda used, and she's my friend, so I said okay. However, this seems to be **NOT OKAY** according to Liz. Liz is in my room now making bracelets with me, and Liz is very **(VERY)** mad. She is telling me how she is feeling while waving her hands a lot as she talks. "You **can't** just **give away** our bracelets!" Liz is saying. "Why?" I say. "You gave your sister, Rachel, a free one." "That's different," says Liz. "Rachel is my sister." "Well," I say. "**Vicki is a good friend.**" "Yeah, as if," says Liz. "Does Vicki ever call you just to say **absolutely nothing?**" "Huh?" I say. **So Liz says...**

• "For me, a **good friend** is someone who calls you to say absolutely nothing-because they want absolutely nothing from you. Just ~~to be your friend~~. And it seems like the <u>ONLY time</u> Vicki calls you is when she wants something, like help with her math homework." • "Um," I say. • "I don't tRust Vicki," Liz continues. "She is not a nice person. She's **mean** to a lot of people at school, which also makes Vicki a big hypocrite, because she has this big sticker on her notebook that says: **MEAN PEOPLE SUCK.**" • Hmmm. • Maybe Liz has a teeny-tiny bead-size point. • Sometimes Vicki **is** mean to some people. • But Vicki doesn't mean **to be mean**. She's just picky about who she lets into her cliques.

You see, there are these **cliques** in school. And you have to be just like the people in the clique to get in the *clique*. If you are different, then you must find a clique of people just like **YOU**. • Actually, it's a lot like how it is in the animal kingdom. I've read that animals have cliques, too. • Certain **FISH** will only swim with certain **FISH**. • Certain *birds* will only fly with certain *birds*. • certain **horses** will only gallop with certain **horses**. • And in our school, the **JOCKS** hang out with the **JOCKS**. • The *artsy kids* hang out with the *artsy kids*. The *cool kids* hang out with *cool kids*. • **MY PROBLEM?**

• I don't just have **one clique** I hang out with. I mainly hang out with Liz. We are our own **two-person clique**. Sometimes I wish I were in a **real** clique, only I don't even know which clique I'd want to be in. • I **guess** I want to be in Vicki's **cool** clique. But I also want to be in the **artsy** clique and the **honors?** club clique.
• I have sooo many different kinds of people inside me. And I **never** know who I am going to be and when. With some people I am

loud. With others I am quiet. With some I feel totally cool. With others I feel like a big geek. • Is it good to be so many different people? • Or is it bad? **And why is it?** • Sometimes I just change without even trying. • Maybe this, too, is an animal instinct thingie. • I've read how some animals can change to match up with whoever they are with.

Like if a chameleon were near a leopard, it would get spots. • Many fish have developed this thing where they first send out vibrations to see if you are in their **"special fish clique,"** and if you are, you have to learn how to send back the same **"special top secret fish clique vibrations."** If you do, then they let you swim with them. • If you are left out. • I relate. feel like I • I sometimes am trying to send out **"special** **top secret clique vibrations,"** with whatever clique I am with so I will not be left out. • So, I act more "*artsy*" when I am with my "*artsy*" friends - and more "*cool*" whenever I am hanging out with Vicki and her clique of *cool friends*. • I wish I didn't →

...care what people think about me. Is that stupid?

Ooops. I just cared what people think about me - again!

Liz **never** cares what people think about her. Liz just cares about being Liz. **So Liz is always just Liz**, no matter who she is with. I wish I could be more like Liz. But then I would not be me, I'd be Liz... **Oh, I think my brain is going to explode!!!**

Liz is more daring than me. For instance, Liz has three piercings in her right ear-lobe. And Liz wants to get a tattoo of a butterfly and maybe a bellybutton piercing - **but I would never have the guts.**

"Why not?" Liz has asked me.

"I'm afraid of what people would say - what my parents would say."

"Well, if you want something deeply in your heart," Liz said, "**then you must follow your heart!**"

Liz is always telling me

I MUST FOLLOW MY HEART.

And I **want** to follow my heart. But sometimes I feel my heart is walking in a circle or a zigzag, and it's hard to follow my heart when it is going **so quickly all over the place**... here... No there... No over there... Yeesh. My heart seems to be **lost** a lot of the time. I guess this is why I don't KNOW which clique I fit into... **and if I fit in anywhere!** I guess I don't really KNOW myself at all! And if **I** don't KNOW **me**, — and I spend soooo much time with me – theN... well... is it possible for **anybody** else to really KNOW me, either? **HELP!**

Note: I think Liz is better at not caring what people think because she already faced one of the **scariest** things ever — watching her mom die. **Wow, huh?** I guess for Liz, after going through something as scary as that, **everything else** feels a lot less scary. (Or at least that's what my mom guesses. My mom once told me that she thinks Liz is very gutsy because this **sad thing** made her **strong inside.** maybe. Liz **is** one of the <u>**gutsiest**</u> people I know. I'm thinking about this when...

... the phone rings snapping me out of my thoughts.

I pick up.

"Hi, it's Vicki," says Vicki.

"Hi, Vicki," I say.

I give Liz this look— a look that says: **see, Vicki is my pal.** She's calling me just to talk. See?

SEE? SEE? SEE?

"How you doing?" asks Vicki.

"Good. And you?" I say.

"Good," says Vicki.

I keep staring at Liz and thinking:

SEE? SEE? SEE?

"So, I looove my new bracelet," says Vicki.

"Thanks," I say.

"I was wondering if you could give me a few more— for my boyfriend, Steve, and his whole football team, like about ten black and green ones, the same colors in their football jerseys," says Vicki.

"You want ten more bracelets?" I say.

I look at Liz again, only this time I am thinking: **uh-oh.**

Maybe Liz is right.

Maybe Vicki just **fakes** being **nice** when she wants something.

Hmmm.

Could it be?

I take a deep breath. "Vicki," I say. "I was thinking. I know I gave you that one bracelet for free."

"And I **loooove** it. It's sooo pretty," says Vicki.

"Thanks," I say, "but I was thinking... I am actually in business with Liz to sell these bracelets so we can make money to buy new computers. So, well, I'm going to have to charge you for any more bracelets. Especially since you want a lot of them."

"**Charge me?**" Vicki says.

"Yeah. It's only fair. I mean, well, I think you should sorta kinda pay for them like everyone else at school."

"Oh," says Vicki.

There's a <u>long</u> silence on the phone.

"Okay. Fine. Sure. Whatever," says Vicki.

"Thanks," I say. "You **do** understand, right?"

"Whatever." says Vicki.

But I have **no idea** what Vicki is thinking or feeling right now.

"Are you mad at me?" I ask.

What is Sweet?

☒ yes

cherry

no ☒

olive

yes no ☒

Vicki

"No sweetie," she says in a voice that is **sooo sweet**, it doesn't sound sweet at all. "So, anyway, gotta go."

"But...I..."

CLICK. Too late. She's hung up.

Ugh. Is Vicki just **faking being sweet** to me? Is Vicki going to run off and talk about me behind my back? Does Vicki still want to be my friend?

I **never** have any of these questions about Liz. I never feel like Liz is being fake nice. I **always** know just how Liz is feeling. Even if she's not feeling so good about me.

When Liz is angry, she tells me she's angry.

When Liz thinks I'm being an idiot because I give away free bracelets, she tells me I'm being an idiot.

"Hey, Liz," I say.

"Yeah," says Liz.

"I just figured out what to look for **most** in a friend."

"Do tell," says Liz raising one eyebrow.

"Someone who is truthful," I say. "**People** who say **truthful things** are the bestest, coolest friends to have."

Liz looks at me and smiles. "And," says Liz, people who say something like that also are the **bestest, coolest friends.**"

"**And** so are people who say something like that **right back**," I say.

"**And** so are people who say something like that **right back** at someone who said something **right back.**"

"**And** so are people who say something like that **right back** at someone who just said—"

"Oh, **SHUT UP!**" Liz says. "You're starting to get on my nerves."

Okay.

So, remember back in the beginning, how my dad promised he'd answer my questions LATER? Well, I feel a lot of laters have already passed—WOOOSH right by—and my dad has yet to answer any questions! My dad has yet to tell me, why, in books a dog has four ways to talk: ①arf ②woof ③bow-wow ④ruff. But a pig only says:①oink. And a cow only says:①moooo. And my dad has yet to tell me why people say they have a frog in their throat...

And my dad has yet to tell me... I love you, Alexandra. ...oops... I know that was **not a** question. That was a statement. But it's a statement I sometimes sorta kinda question. (uh-oh. Just thinking about it now gives me a ← **PORCUPINE** in my throat !)

...and butterflies in their tummy, why not a **PORCUPINE IN THEIR THROAT,** and armadillos in their tummy?

I know, I know, I know, I **Know.** (I even **KNOW**!) My mom has explained this all to me a gazillion times: My dad (says my mom) is just not the type to say "mushy-gushy-love-things." My dad (says my mom) is just not a mushy-gushy kinda guy. He's a senior V.P. in charge of marketing. Whatever that means. Actually, what it means is: He works really, really hard. So I barely get to talk to him. And when my dad does have time to talk, what he most wants to talk about is...

BASKET-BALL.

"Oakley's gonna chew up Barkley when Phoenix..."

comes to town," says my dad to my brother, Howie. • "It's a slam dunk," Howie agrees. • I want to join in as they watch and talk about the game, but it's like they're speaking a foreign language. They might as well be saying: "Ishkabibble scoobibabble." • I know nothing about sports. But I know all about animals. • "Hey, Dad," I say, "I know what I want to be when I grow up — a veterinarian." • "Yes!" says my dad, "Yes! It's a rimshot! Score!" • Sometimes I feel the only way to get my dad's attention is to become a **forward** on the **New York Knicks.**

Unfortunately, I'm only 4 foot 11 — in Rollerblades. I most likely would have a hard time passing the Knicks' height requirement.

.Though I feel silly complaining about my dad. I know there are dads who are much (much) worse. I've seen Ricki Lake. I don't think my complaints about my dad would even register on **the Ricki Lake** "gasp-o-meter." I don't know. I don't know **how I feel.** or how I **should** feel. Or **how I feel** about **how I should** feel. I think I feel... like **choco-late.** In particular, I'm **craving** Big Bob's **choco-chunk cookies.** I head into the kitchen—

-**"WAIT"** says my dad. "Put that cookie down!! We're heading out to dinner tonight. Just you and me." "What?" I say. "your mom has sing-ing rehearsal, and Howie has basketball practice," says my dad "So it's just us to-night. **Where** do you

BIG BOB'S CHOCO-CHUNK

ANTONIO'S CALAMARI

want to go?". "Um, how about **Antonio's**?" I suggest. "They have the best crispy calamari!". "Mm-mmm **crispy calamari**," my dad and I say — at **the same time!** At last, a topic we agree on: crispy calamari. Not much, but it's a start. "I'll get my coat," I tell my dad, my crispy calamari partner. "Honey,"

says my dad, "are you sure you can eat calamari?". "What?". "Didn't you tell me you wanted to be a vegetarian?" he says. "A what?". "A vegetarian," he repeats. "No, no!" I say. "I said **veterinarian!**". I wonder: will my dad and I ever be able to communicate? **Am I talking in a voice only elves can hear?**. Who knows. Maybe tonight will be different. I know it's only one small meal, yet on some level I'm hoping to create a food bonding experience that will match Little League games everywhere.

We hear you!

Then finally it happens. **Here I am, with my dad, now, at Antonio's, talking at last.**

   Sort of talking.

   "New menu," says my dad.

   "Looks good," I say.

   I am trying to think up things to talk about. Rollerblading? Naaah. Computer games? Uh, don't think so. The difference between amphibians and mammals? Hmm, nope. Uh-oh. What do my dad and I have to say to each other?

I butter my bread.

I study my water.

I stare at a lady's weird hairdo.

I look down at my shoes.

• My dad and I have lived in a house 🏠 **together** for 12 ½th years, yet we hardly know each other. I flip through the **photo album** 🖼🖼🖼 **of my mind** for **shared moments.** but they're all of: Mom or Howie, Mom, Mom, Howie, Mom, Howie, Howie, Mom, Howie, Mom. **Then finally** I locate **a Dad memory.** 💡 "Hey, Dad, remember the time I visited you in your office?" I say. "I remember the **swivel chairs** 🪑, the **elecfRonic pencil sharpeners** 〰, the colored pencils, the **XeRox machine** 🌼🌼🌼. And I remember how at the end of the day you pRomised me if I were good, you'd get me **a gift.** 🎁. 'How about **a pet?**" I asked you. And you said **okay.** ☺ So, I of course pictured getting a . . .

...a PUPPY.

"Yeah, now I remember," says my dad. "And how in the middle of the day you tugged me on the pant leg and asked, 'How am I doing so far, Daddy? Am I doing okay?' **You were so cute**, I just wanted to reach down and **hug you**." • "So, why didn't you, Dad?" "Didn't I what?" • "Hug me." • "You KNOW, I don't know," he says. • He **tries to smile**, but just like that hug, it never quite comes. • I'm sad/angry/amused/bitter. I want to blurt out everything

I'm feeling, but my **lips feel frozen shut.** I'm as bad as him, I suppose, not being able to say what I feel. But I'm **just** the **daughter.** He's **"The Dad."** He's older and should be better at this, right?

"Do you know what you want?"

I look up. It's the waiter.

"Do you know what you want?" he repeats.

"I'm not sure," I say.

My response echoes **with mega-meaning.** What do I want? I had big expectations for my dad and dinner tonight— for us to be like other fathers and daughters. Now I wonder how **one small meal** can fill all the hunger inside me.

"Want to start with the **fried calamari?"** my dad asks.

"Uh, no. Not tonight," I say.

It's not that I don't want the fried calamari. I **fear it.** Ordering an appetizer would mean an extra half hour of conversation that my dad and I would have to fill and thereby remind us that he and I have nothing to say to each other. In a word: **YIKES!**

"Hey, remember when we went fishing?" my dad asks. • "What? Dad, we never went fishing," I say, annoyed • "I'm kind of joking," says my dad. "I meant at that pet store, later that night, after your office visit when we got to the pet store, you got to pick out pet fish. You were so happy, remember?" • But what I remember is wondering: FISH? I mean, no way does **a fish = a puppy**. 100 fish ≠ 1 puppy. 100 fish ≠ ½ puppy. All I wanted was **1 PUPPY!** I mean, was my dad kidding? • But

...he wasn't. • The next thing I knew I had 2 new fish room-mates: **SPOT** and **SPOTCUBED**, named after their unique markings. SPOT wore this **bizarre spot** across his face. And SPOT CUBED wore three odd spots **on his left —** or would that be his **right?** — side.

I was bummed I was only getting fish, but I was **psyched** to spend time with my dad.

I was amazed my dad had time to mull over the pros and cons of **blue** VS green tiny, shrunken treasure chests.

And **pink** VS **purple pebbles**. And **square** VS **round aquariums**. It made me soooo happy: the sight of a tiny, pretty **plastic mermaid** lying there in the palm of my dad's large hand. Then, when I got home, I had the **strangest re-action**.

• I wanted those fish to **die, die, die.** • And quickly. • I hated those fish because they weren't puppies. You can't take a fish for a walk. Or teach a fish any tricks. Except maybe play dead. Fish do that trick well. **EXCEPT MY FISH**. They just would not die. Even after months and months of barely changing their water. • My goal, of course, was for them to choke to death. • I still wanted a **PUPPY-** **a puppy who** love me, lick

HEEL
PLAY DEAD
CATCH

would me, wag **happily at the sight of me.** I hated those fish for pretending to be pets, for fooling my dad into thinking that the tiny bit of love and attention they offered would be enough. • (**Note:** I wanted more love from a pet. I LOVE LOVE! How come my dad could not see that? Know that? Give me that?) • Soon I had nightmares. I dreamed my **FISH GREW LOCH NESS MONSTER SIZED AND SOUGHT REVENGE ON ME FOR NOT LOVING THEM AS THEY WERE.**

"Yeah," says my dad, smiling at me from across the dinner table. "Yeah, you sure loved those fish. I remember, when you went to camp, how much you missed them. You'd write asking about them."

But what I remember is writing, hoping I'd receive back a fish obituary.

"I remember," says my dad, "how **unhappy** you were when you found them, you know, passed on."

But what I remember is thinking that was the **happiest** day of my young life.

"I know," says my dad, "why don't I buy you some more goldfish after dinner?"

"Well, I..."

"Oh, wait, I can't. I have to work. But let me give you some money, and you can pick some up tomorrow."

"No thanks."

"Please, take it."

"No!"

"Really. My treat."

"**NO !!**"

"What?" says my dad, shocked by the extreme **NO-ness** of my response. →

"I have something to admit," I say. "I hated those fish. I always wanted them to die. I hated them because

they weren't puppies. That's why I never changed their water—I

was hoping they'd choke to death. But those fish were, like, bionic. They must have lived for three years!! I was ready to contact Guiness Book of World Records!"

Dad sits back and looks at me. "I have something to admit, too," he says. "That summer you went to camp, those fish did die. And sometimes when you didn't change the water, I would. And I'd find them dead, and each time I'd replace them because I thought you loved them so much." →

"No," I say. "NO WAY! I would have noticed! Those fish had **BIZARRE** markings!"

"Well," my dad chuckles, "that's because I made the salesman find fish that looked exactly like Spot and Spot Cubed." • And I picture my dad, a man with a very busy schedule—

—I picture him standing in front of that huge fish tank, filled with hundreds, if not thousands, of fish, and him saying to the salesguy, who has this teeny tiny net,